PELLY

Dave Glaze

COTEAU BOOKS

Edited by Barbara Sapergia.
Cover and text illustrations by Bill Johnson.
Cover design by Bill Johnson.
Book design and typesetting by Val Jakubowski.
Printed and bound in Canada at Transcontinental Printing Inc.

The publisher gratefully acknowledges the financial assistance
of the Saskatchewan Arts Board, the Canada Council, and the
Department of Communications.

Canadian Cataloguing in Publication Data

Glaze, Dave, 1947-

   Pelly

   ISBN 1-55050-049-X

I. Pelicans - Juvenile fiction. I. Johnson, Bill.
II. Title.
PS8563.L39P44 1993   jC813'.54   C93-098026-3
PZ7.G43Pe 1993

COTEAU BOOKS
401 - 2206 Dewdney Ave
Regina, Saskatchewan
Canada S4R 1H3

For Sarah and Alice

Chapter 1

The redheaded boy jumped off his bike and let it fall to the dirt path. On either side, tangled tree branches climbed over his head. "Down here," he called, waving to his two friends. Without waiting for the others to lay down their bikes, he pushed aside the branches and started down the steep riverbank.

Moments later he stepped into a clearing and looked down a waterfall. The waterfall was formed by a three-metre-high wall, or weir, built across the river underwater.

"There," the redhead said as his friends caught up with him. "That's what I'm talking about."

A flock of thirty white pelicans swam in the heaving waves below the waterfall. With their wings tucked up along their backs, the birds paddled slowly in search of fish. The tips of their long, orange bills cut through the water.

"If we could bag those suckers, we'd be rich," the redhead said. He was shorter than either of his friends. Although the temperature was barely ten above, he wore only a T-shirt and blue jeans. The other two wore fall jackets.

"What do you mean?" one of the friends asked. "Those are just pelicans." He tugged the back of his jacket over a strip of bare skin above his jeans. "They're nothing special."

"Depends who wants them," the redhead said. "My uncle stuffs animals – you know, for hunters. They pay him to stuff what they shoot. And sometimes they want to buy things they didn't even get themselves. Like a pelican."

"He'd stuff a pelican?"

"Sure. And he gets lots of money for them, too, because guys can't shoot them."

"How much?"

"Three hundred dollars, maybe," the redhead said. "And he'll give me twenty-five for every pelican I bring him."

"Twenty-five bucks! Geez, I'd pop one off for that."

"Dream on," the third friend said. She had been standing with her hands shoved into her pockets while the two boys talked. "You won't even get close to those pelicans. They always stay out in the middle of the river."

The redhead turned to her. "We'll do it," he said. "I'll think of something."

"Yeah," the other boy said. "For that much money I might even get my feet wet."

"Come on," the redhead said. "We'll go to my place and make a plan." He turned and led the other two back up the hill to their bikes.

On the other side of the water, the riverbank was a park, with paved pathways and flattened hills covered with lawns. A high chain link and barbed wire fence kept people from the waterfall. Here, hidden in a clump of reeds near the end of the weir, another girl squatted in the mud.

For two hours Sandra had been watching the pelicans. At first the weak September sun had warmed her back, but now the riverbank was in shadow. Cold river water had seeped into her runners, and Sandra could feel the chill creeping up her legs. A puff of wind blew her hair over her face. Carefully she reached one hand up to her forehead and tucked the straight, long hair behind one ear and then the other.

Near the shore, a young female pelican jabbed her head underwater. Her black-tipped wings whipped out flat to her sides.

Sandra pretended she was underwater with the pelican. A jackfish flitted toward her. Opening her bill, she plunged deeper into the river. When the fish swam closer, she clamped shut her bill and kicked back to the surface.

As the pelican held her bill out across the water, Sandra saw the loose skin of the pouch flapping. The bill jerked upwards then settled back down.

"Got another one! Good for you!" she whispered.

In one motion all of the birds turned away from the waterfall. Sandra hadn't seen or heard any signal pass between them. The young pelican, the one Sandra had been watching, paddled to the end of the weir. Sandra sucked in her breath. This was what she had been waiting for.

About two metres from shore, the pelican stopped swimming and let herself drift downstream, toward Sandra. When she reached the girl, the pelican turned around to face against the current. Staring at Sandra, the bird paddled her big webbed feet to stay in one spot.

"Hi, pelican. Thanks for coming to see me again." Sandra spoke softly.

The pelican's long neck curled up from her body. Tucked against her neck, her bill was flat and hard on top, with a ridge running up the middle. Circling the eyes at the top of the bill was a patch of bright yellow skin. The tip of the bill reached almost to the water.

Sandra smiled. "When you're fishing, you look like someone bobbing for apples. You know, when you put your wings out like this – and stick your head under the water."

As she spoke, Sandra threw her arms out to her sides. The pelican beat her wings and pushed herself away from the riverbank. Sandra gasped, "Oh, I'm sorry."

Slowly she lowered her arms and sat very still. She waited before she spoke again. "I've got more stuff for you."

Drawing a hand from a pocket of her jacket, Sandra reached out toward the bird. With unblinking eyes, the pelican watched Sandra drop pieces of popcorn onto the water. By twisting and stretching her neck, the pelican snatched up each little puff.

"You like this, don't you?" Sandra said, sprinkling more popcorn on the water. "But that's all there is."

After wiping her hands on her jeans, she hugged her arms around her knees. The pelican arched her neck and partly spread her wings. She seemed to lift herself almost out of the water.

"Wow, are your wings ever huge!" Sandra exclaimed softly. "And you didn't even open them all the way."

The pelican floated further down the river, away from the girl. Smiling, Sandra stood up and looked at her watch. It was almost four o'clock. She'd have to run. If she was very late, her father might not let her come back to the river tomorrow.

Chapter 2

Sandra and her father, Wesley, had been living in Saskatoon for a month. Their apartment, on the third floor of a yellow brick building, had two small bedrooms, a tiny kitchen, and a living-room.

Wesley was reading the newspaper when Sandra got home. She stopped just inside the door as Wesley dropped the paper onto his lap.

"She came again!" Sandra cried.

"What?" her father asked, smoothing his moustache over his upper lip. "Who came again?"

"The little pelican, the one I've been watching, she came right up to me again!" Sandra kicked off her running shoes and unzipped her jacket. "At first she just looked at me. Then I talked to her really quietly, and she ate the popcorn I gave her. And then she waved her wings at me and floated off. She's never waved like that before. You should see her wings!" Sandra sat on the arm of the couch.

"Really?" Looking up at his daughter, Wesley smiled. "Boy, that's something, kid."

"She's so pretty when you see her close up." Sandra got up from the couch as she talked. "Her feathers aren't all white. The ones at the back of her head and neck are kind of grey. and she has browny-grey freckles along the tops of her wings. And her chest feathers look as if they've been smudged with yellow chalk or something. It's really neat."

"Sounds like it might be a young one," Wesley said. "Sometimes their colouring is a bit different."

""Maybe. Anyway, come with me tomorrow to see her, okay?"

"Uh, we'll see," Wesley said. "How do you know it's a she, anyway?"

"Well, I don't really know, of course," Sandra answered. "That's just what I think."

"Have you given her a name?" Wesley asked.

"No, I'll have to think of one, I guess." Sandra was quiet for a moment. "So, will you come? Tomorrow?"

Wesley frowned and looked down at his paper.

"Just for a little while," Sandra persisted.

"You think it'll really come this time?" Wesley asked. "It never has before when I've been with you."

"I know," Sandra answered. "But I'm sure she'll come again tomorrow, and I really want you to see her."

"Okay," Wesley said. "I'll go down with you in the morning."

"Thank you, Daddy," Sandra said, falling backwards onto the couch cushions. "I'm sorry I'm late.

She came just when it was time to go. Then I ran all the way home."

"That's all right," her father replied, you were close enough."

When Wesley started reading again, Sandra looked around the room. The furniture was theirs, and her school picture was on the wall, but the apartment still felt strange to her. Her real home was in Big River, a little town about two hundred and fifty kilometres north of the city. She'd lived there all her life.

Sandra's mother had died when Sandra was born. Until she started school, Sandra had been looked after by her Grandma Betty, Wesley's mother. Then she and her father had moved down the street a ways, to their own house.

For as long as Sandra could remember, her father had worked at a sawmill in town. When the mill closed down, Wesley decided to move to Saskatoon so he could take a carpentry course. Sandra had wanted to stay with her grandmother, but Wesley wouldn't allow it.

Sandra didn't know anyone to play with in the city. Before his course began, Wesley took her the few blocks to see the river. Afterwards, even after school started, she kept going to the riverbank on her own. When the pelicans arrived, she visited them every day.

One time she started to tell a girl in her class how she liked to spend time near the pelicans.

"Really?" the girl asked.

"Sure," Sandra said. "Have you ever seen the pelicans?"

"Of course, we drive by there all the time. They're not so exciting." The girl laughed a little and raised her eyebrows. "You mean every day you go down to the river and watch those birds?"

"It's fun," Sandra said, "and they're not just any birds. Pelicans are really amazing when you see them close up. There's this one who comes right up to me so I can feed her."

"Well, aren't you lucky!" the girl rolled her eyes and turned away. After that, Sandra hadn't tried to tell anyone else about the pelicans.

Sandra frowned at the memory. People said she looked like her dad when she did that. Without changing her expression, Sandra felt the wrinkles in the middle of her forehead. She tried to flatten the skin with her fingers, but the little ridges kept coming back. It means you worry too much, her grandmother said.

Wesley's face was hidden behind the newspaper, but Sandra knew his forehead would be wrinkled, too. It had been like that a lot since they moved to Saskatoon.

Sandra wasn't thinking about the girl's unkind words the next day as she led Wesley to the weir. Squeezing the bread crumbs in her jacket pocket, she had to force herself to walk at her father's slow pace.

"You really like coming here, don't you?" Wesley asked.

"It's the best place, Daddy," Sandra said. "When you're down in the bushes and all you can see is the water and the trees on the other side, it's like you're not even in the city. And when you get near the waterfall, you can't hear the cars or anything."

"Sort of like back at Big River?"

"Sort of," Sandra said. "Except there I wouldn't be alone."

"That's true," Wesley agreed. He looked further along the pathway. "You don't see many people down here. Not like in the summer."

A cold north wind swirled down the river valley. Like penguins riding an ice floe, the pelicans huddled together on a sandbar. Pointing to a pelican at one end of the flock, Sandra whispered to her dad. "There she is. We just have to wait here until she comes."

Wesley started to say something, then stopped. Five or six times he had come with Sandra to the river. Not once had any pelican come close to them. After a few minutes, he shivered and rubbed his hands together. "It's colder than I thought down here," he said.

"Sshhh," Sandra answered, without moving.

"We should go across to the other side of the river sometime," Wesley said, jabbing his hand in that direction. "See what it's like over there."

"Daddy, please," Sandra said in a hushed voice, "we have to be quiet." She kept her back to Wesley so she could watch the pelicans.

"We could go across that railway bridge," Wesley said in a forced whisper. He tapped Sandra on the shoulder and pointed to an iron bridge about two hundred metres down the river.

"I don't want to go across that bridge!" Sandra shook her head. "There's just a little wooden sidewalk for people to walk on. I'd be too scared."

A few more minutes went by. "I don't know," Wesley said. "Those pelicans look like they're going to stay pretty close together, just to keep warm. Let's give them a bit longer and then go home for lunch. So we can warm up too."

Sandra sighed. Her father was right, her pelican probably wouldn't leave the sandbar. But Wesley hadn't helped by talking and moving around.

"I want to come back again after lunch. Can I?" Sandra asked. "I don't know," Wesley said. "I can't come back with you. I've got work to do." He looked up at some dark clouds approaching the city. "I guess you can come back for a couple of hours, if you dress warmly. But you have to leave right away if it starts to rain."

"Okay," Sandra said. "I'll get her to come to me somehow."

"Sure," Wesley said, "you let me know."

When she returned after lunch, the pelicans were fishing together. After another hour of waiting, Sandra saw the flock turn away from the waterfall. A lone bird paddled toward her. For a few moments the pelican and the girl stared at one another.

"Hi, pelican," Sandra said quietly, "I'm glad you came to see me again." Sandra slipped a hand into her jacket pocket, then reached out toward the pelican. "Here, try some of this." The pelican swam closer and snatched the pieces of bread as Sandra dropped them onto the water.

The wind pushing against Sandra's face seemed to falter. She looked up. A grey curtain of mist was drawing toward her along the river. As she watched, the curtain fell around the railway bridge. Sandra felt the first cold drops on her face.

"Aw! Now I'll have to go home. Well, at least you got here before it started to rain."

The scattered drops became a light drizzle as

Sandra laid the rest of the crumbs in front of the
waiting bird. A gust of wind pushed the rain up
Sandra's sleeves and down the back of her neck.
She shoved wet strands of hair behind her ears.

Standing up slowly, Sandra spread her arms out
at her sides. The young pelican arched out of the
water and partly opened her wings. Shivering,
Sandra turned and pushed through the reeds.
When she reached the top of the riverbank, she
looked back and waved goodbye.

The pelican turned toward the waterfall.
Swimming near the shore, the bird poked at bits of
paper and soggy cigarettes. At the base of the falls,
she found jackfish struggling to escape from a shallow pool in some rocks. The pelican leaned forward
and scooped the fish into her bill.

Chapter 3

Day after day the sky was clear and the air very cold. Inside Sandra's school the radiators hissed and banged and gave off a warm musty smell.

The windows in her classroom faced the river. Because it was a few blocks away, Sandra couldn't see the river, only the trees on the shore.

When she noticed the first few pelicans, they looked like little white clouds far away. The clouds were making tiny circles in the sky. More clouds joined them.

Sandra glanced at her teacher's desk which was circled with students waiting for notebooks to be marked. She walked to the windows.

The pelicans were leaving the river. Lifting into the air in a closely spaced line, the birds rose to the north, into the wind. They turned to the west and then to the south, flying right over the school yard and back across the river. Flap, flap, flap. Six or seven times the whole line of pelicans beat their wings in unison before gliding on an air current. Then more wingbeats, all in time with the leader.

Everyone's in step, just like in a parade, Sandra thought. She could see that each bird had its neck doubled back and its feet tucked in. Sandra watched the flock until it was lost from sight behind some tall trees on the far riverbank.

The hours dragged by until she was back in the apartment with her father. "They flew right over the school," she told Wesley. "so I got to say goodbuye to them."

"Hey, that's great," he said.

"I thought I'd be able to tell the one I've been feeding," Sandra went on, "but I couldn't. They all look too much alike when they're flying."

"I guess so." Wesley looked thoughtful as he pulled gently on the hairs of his moustache. "Now that the pelicans have gone," he said, "I don't want you going to the river any more. There's nobody down there these days. It's not too safe for a girl by herself."

Sandra shrugged. "It's no fun when it's so cold, anyway." Then she added, "Except, can I go once more, on Saturday, just for one last quick visit?"

"All right," Wesley agreed, "once more. but then it's time for you to get some real friends."

On Saturday Sandra wore her winter jacket and mitts. No-one was in the park as she hurried to the patch of reeds where she had fed the pelican. Slipping through the brittle stalks, Sandra crouched in the hardened mud.

Closing her eyes, she remembered how the young pelican had paddled close enough to pick up the bread crumbs she'd dropped. Sandra held her hand over the water the way she would if the bird were really there. She imagined how the bird's hard bill would feel as it nudged her hand. The bill felt almost real. Sandra opened her eyes.

A pelican pushed away from her outstretched hand. When just out of reach, the pelican dropped its bill onto its neck and stared at her.

"Pelly!" she exclaimed. "Is that you? I thought you left!"

Sandra squinted at the bird. It looked like the same pelican. Standing up slowly, she stretched her arms to her sides. The pelican arched out of the water enough to show her black wingtips. Delighted, Sandra crouched down again and grinned at her good luck.

"It is you! And I've given you a name. Pelly. I like it. And now you're going to stay and be my friend."

The smile on Sandra's face faded to a frown. Pelly couldn't stay there and be her friend. The bird wouldn't survive the winter. Soon the whole river would be hidden under a thick layer of ice.

"Pelly, what happened?" Sandra asked out loud. "Why didn't you go? Did you think I was going to feed you? Is that why you stayed?" Sandra shook her head. "I can't feed you through the winter, you goof! I didn't even bring anything for you to eat today!"

Sandra's arms curled around her legs. For a long time she stared at the big bird bobbing calmly on the waves. Taking a deep breath, she stood up. "I've got to go now, Pelly," she said. "This is so weird! I'm not even supposed to come back here any more."

On the way home, Sandra decided she would keep feeding Pelly. But she wouldn't tell her father. She knew Wesley didn't believe there was a special pelican. When Pelly was really tame, Sandra would get her father to come back to the river with her.

Shortly after one of Sandra's visits, Pelly swam up to some other children walking along the shore. The pelican stopped near them, and stared. She opened and shut her bill.

"Is it ever pretty," the girl whispered. She crouched in the mud by the water and looked closely at Pelly. "Look at her long neck."

"Yeah, I'd like to get my hands on that neck," one boy said. "Twenty-five bucks, right?"

The redhead nodded. "Right. Now's our chance. Where's something we can hit it with?" Turning away from the river, he said to the other boy, "Get me that stick."

"How're you going to get close enough to hit it?" the boy asked. He handed the redhead a branch the size of a baseball bat.

"Try and get it to come to you," the redhead told the girl.

She held her hand out across the water and waved her fingers. "Come, pelican," she called. "Come here," She shook her head. "It's not going to come any closer. It's too smart."

"Birds aren't smart," the redhead said. "And you didn't try very hard." He threw the branch behind him on the riverbank. "Grab some rocks. If we stun it, we could grab it and pull the sucker out of the water." The two boys picked up a handful of stones each. The redhead nudged the girl and held out a rock to her. "Ready?" he asked, as he turned the biggest rock over in his hand. "Aim for the head."

The three children pulled their arms back sharply and threw their stones. Startled by the sudden movement, Pelly beat her wings backwards. One stone struck her wing. The others splashed around her.

With quick wingbeats, the pelican lifted out of

the water. Hanging below her body, her legs jerked with each beat of her wings. A few more powerful strokes and she tucked her legs into her underside.

"Geez, you guys couldn't even hit it," the red-head cried angrily.

"That was my rock that hit it!" the other boy complained.

The girl didn't look at the two boys. She squatted down in the mud again and watched the pelican skim just above the water to the other side of the river.

Chapter 4

A plastic bird feeder hung from a tree that stood behind Sandra's apartment building. By kneeling against the back of the couch, Sandra could look out the window and spy on the hungry birds. She liked to watch the fussy sparrows flick the shells of sunflower seeds onto the ground.

In a flurry of wings, the sparrows suddenly scattered. Pushing herself further up the back of the couch, Sandra peered down to the base of the tree. A long-haired yellow cat was slowly clawing his way up the trunk.

The cat crept along a branch until he was right above the bird feeder. Curling his head and one paw around the branch, he jabbed at the feeder. A claw caught the wire holding the feeder and sent it swinging wildly.

For a few seconds the cat didn't move. Then, he

turned and walked back along the branch. After going down on his haunches, the cat jumped straight up to catch onto the trunk. He climbed to another branch. There he sat, slowly turning his head to peer around the tree. Almost at eye level with Sandra, the cat looked her way "Mmrrrup!" he called.

"Kittykittykitty! Come on down!" a voice urged. "Come on. The birds are all gone. Kittykittykitty-kitty."

Sandra pressed her face against the window so she could see down to the ground. A boy about her own age stood near the bottom of the tree. "Come on, No Pets, don't be so stupid. Get down."

Sandra knew that the boy and his younger brother had just moved into the apartment building. They lived with their mother.

"Where is he, Jason?" The voice of the little brother carried up to Sandra.

"Up on that branch," Jason pointed. "I think the dummy's getting ready to jump."

Sandra saw the cat swishing his tail sharply. A sparrow had perched on the feeder.

"Don't jump, No Pets. You'll never get it!" Jason shouted.

The cat sprang from the branch. Like a trapeze artist in a circus, he sailed through the air with outstretched paws. Sandra couldn't tell how close the cat came, but he missed the bird feeder. The sparrow flew off unharmed.

With his paws still stretched out front and back, the cat struck the earth and lay without moving. Sandra saw Jason and his little bother start toward the cat. She slipped off the couch and ran out of her apartment.

When she reached the boys, the cat was hanging

limply over Jason's arm.

"Is he hurt?" Sandra asked.

"No Pets? No, he does that all the time. He's not too bright, but he is pretty tough." Jason bounced the cat on his arms. "Now he'll play dead for awhile. He likes the attention."

"What did you call him?" Sandra asked.

"No Pets," Jason said, "you know, like on the sign." He glanced at a notice stuck on the back door. NO PETS ALLOWED, it read.

"My mom says that's always the rule any place we stay," Jason said. "so when we found this guy, we named him No Pets, so we could keep him."

Sandra saw the tip of the cat's tail flick a little. She reached over and stroked his fur. The cat tried to draw his paws up onto Jason's arm.

"See, that's all he wanted," Jason said. "Here, do you want to hold him?"

Pulling the cat off Jason's arm, Sandra hung his front paws over her shoulder and held him against her chest. After a few gentle strokes down his body, the cat began to purr.

"Aw, he's nice," she said, laying her head on his back to listen to the purring. When she looked up, the boys were staring at her. With the same brown eyes and round faces, it was easy to tell the two were brothers.

Jason introduced himself. "And this is my brother, Robert," he added.

Sandra put the cat on the ground. "I'm Sandra," she said. "You guys live here now, don't you?"

On the way into the building to warm up, Sandra learned the boys were going to start at her school after the weekend. Jason would be in her class.

NO PETS
ALLOWED

BY ORDER: The Management

Chapter 5

A city work crew had dug a hole in the street just down from Sandra's apartment building. When the hole was filled in, a tractor's tires had left furrows in the dirt. Rain had gathered in the ruts, and then frozen. Trapped under the blue-green ice were white bubbles of air.

"This one's mine," Sandra called as she ducked under the wooden barrier. Jason and Robert watched as Sandra stomped down on a sheet of ice.

The ice splintered and blotches of muddy water spurted onto her running shoes.

"Hey, let me try that," Robert said. He tapped his foot on another stretch of ice. When it didn't break he jumped down hard with both feet. Mud spattered his pant legs up to his knees. Laughing, Robert slid further down the rut.

When most of the ice had been broken apart, the three children leaned against the barricade.

"There's more stuff like this in the back alley," Jason said. "Let's go smash it, too.

"I can't," Sandra said. "I have to do something."

Robert frowned at her.

"Sorry. I can't come right now, really. I just remembered something I have to do. I'll play with you guys after lunch, okay?"

Sandra turned back to the apartment building. "See you," she called over her shoulder. In her kitchen Sandra found a crumpled bag in the bottom of a box of salted crackers. She pushed the bag into her jacket pocket and hurried out.

Fine white mists swirled over the dark green water of the river. It looked to Sandra like satellite pictures of clouds rushing around the earth. The shallow water near the shore was covered with a rough crust of ice.

When Sandra called, Pelly swam as close to the shore as she could. Stretching her neck and bill over the ice, the pelican picked at the bits of crackers that Sandra threw to her.

"You're doing okay so far, aren't you, Pelly," Sandra said. "When do you think you're going to go someplace warmer?"

Paddling in one spot, the pelican stared at the girl. "You can't stay here, you know," Sandra scolded. "The ice is going to be all across the river."

Pelly began to drift away. She stopped when Sandra stood up. As Sandra went up on tiptoe and stretched out her arms, the pelican arched herself out of the water.

"Maybe I should stop feeding you," Sandra said. "I think I will. I'm not even going to come any more. Maybe then you'll smarten up and leave."

Chapter 6

Drifting below the falls in a search for fish, the pelican plunged completely underwater. In an instant the fast-moving river sucked her beneath a shelf of ice.

When Pelly tried to surface, she struck the rough underside of the ice. Again and again, the sharp ridges scraped along her back as the current pushed her further under the ice.

Tiring and almost out of breath, the pelican kicked herself deeper. Caught suddenly in a cross current, the pelican was pulled across the river. The underwater light brightened. She was out from under the ice. With a feeble kick, Pelly bobbed up to the surface.

The pelican floated motionless on the water until she struck a sandbar. Planting her feet on the shallow bottom, she pulled her chest and neck out of the water. With slow, careful movements, she began to preen her feathers.

As she groomed herself, Pelly was surrounded by a dozen mallard ducks. The birds wore their winter coats of dark and light brown flecked with white. The male mallards stood out because of the deep green feathers on their heads and their white collars.

After clustering around the pelican for a few minutes, the ducks formed a large V in the water. They swam down the river. Like a huge water-skier pulled by tiny boats, the pelican followed in their wakes. Then, leaving twelve frothy trails on the water, the ducks noisily launched themselves into the air. Pelly paddled back to the waterfall.

Sometime in December, ice covered the river completely. Only a narrow strip of wavy water right below the falls stayed clear. Pelly had this to use for fishing.

Chapter 7

Light from the kitchen cast a bright arc into the early morning dark of Sandra's bedroom. When Wesley poked his head into the open doorway, his face was in shadow.

"Sandra?" he whispered, "are you awake? I'm off."

Sandra squinted and held one hand over her eyes. When Wesley's course had finished for the holidays, he'd started working for a carpenter in the city.

"Looks like we're going to get our first big snowstorm today," he went on. "It's already started. Jason's mom said you could go down there this morning if you want. If I'm not home in time, you can have lunch with them, too. She said to tell you it'll be spaghetti. That's your favourite, right?"

Sandra nodded.

"Sorry I have to be away today." Wesley's forehead wrinkled. "When I get paid next week, we'll do our Christmas shopping, okay?"

"Mmmm-hmmm," Sandra murmured.

Wesley leaned over to kiss her. "Go back to sleep now. I'll see you later."

"Bye, Daddy," she said. Then Wesley closed the bedroom door and the room was dark once more. Sandra rolled onto her side and curled up under the covers.

When Sandra woke again it was almost ten o'clock. Out her bedroom window she could see a dull grey cloud that seemed to be hanging just above the apartment building. Millions of tiny snowflakes fell from the cloud.

Jason and Robert were standing in the yard with their backs to the building. As she watched, Jason reached over to take No Pets from Robert's arms. Robert had to pull the cat's paws from his coat.

After quickly pulling on some jeans and a jacket, Sandra ran down to the boys. Snowflakes stuck to their hair like confetti. No Pets tilted his head to the side and swatted at the snow drifting down.

"He won't let go," Jason laughed. "Whenever I try to put him down, he digs his claws in." Jason bounced the cat in his arms. "You take him."

Sandra lifted No Pets onto her shoulder. After stroking his back, she gently lowered him to the ground. No Pets picked up each paw in turn and shook it.

"What a goof!" Jason said. "He's afraid of the snow."

"No," Sandra said, as she scooped up the cat and cuddled him again in her arms. "He just doesn't remember snow from last year. It looks strange to him at first." She put the cat back on the ground.

No Pets shook the snow from his fur. In three quick leaps he was across the yard and part way up the tree. He pulled himself onto one of the bare lower branches.

So thick were the snowflakes that Sandra lost sight of the cat. She wondered, suddenly, what Pelly was thinking about her first snowstorm. The last time she'd checked, the pelican was still at the waterfall. Unlike No Pets, Pelly would have nowhere to hide. And, worse than that, she might be starving. It's probably too late for her to leave now, Sandra thought. I'll have to find some way to keep her alive.

"Hey, Sandra, are you listening?" Jason asked. "Do you want to come?"

Sandra hadn't even heard him talking. Blankly, she looked at Jason, the top of his head now completely white.

"I said, do you want to come to our place?" he asked. "We just got Deadly Destroyer 3. You can play against me."

"What about Robert?" Sandra asked, turning to the younger brother. "Don't you want to play?"

"No, I don't like video games," Robert said. "You guys play. Mom gave me some new felt markers. I'll use them." Robert and Sandra followed Jason into the apartment building.

Three hours later, after eating lunch with the boys, Sandra was slouched in front of the television in her own apartment. A man, dressed in a pirate's costume, was advertising a seafood store. As he walked around the store, he pointed with his sword to trays piled high with different coloured fish fillets.

That's it! Sandra thought. A fish store would have lots of stuff for Pelly.

Long John Silver's Seafood Market was just a few blocks from where Sandra lived. Spread across the large store windows was a painting of an octopus. The octopus was wearing a red toque and holding a wrapped Christmas present in each tentacle.

Stepping inside, Sandra was surrounded by the warm, wet smell of fish. A huge glass water tank stood in the centre of the store. Lining the walls were the steel and glass counters Sandra recognized from the TV ad. Behind the counters, clerks wearing long yellow aprons were helping customers.

Sandra walked to the middle of the room. About twenty green lobsters floated about inside the tank. Streams of bubbles raced up the sides and popped out of the water.

"Can I help you, dear?" The unexpected question made Sandra jump. She turned to face a woman who was wiping the glass front of a nearby counter. As the woman straightened up, she pushed back some hair that had fallen from her bun. The woman was smiling, but to Sandra it didn't look like a friendly smile.

"What is it you want?"

Sandra felt confused. All around her she could see the piles of fish she expected, but she didn't know what anything was called.

"I want some ... fish."

"Yes, well, what kind of fish?" The woman raised her voice as she looked at one of the other clerks. "Do you know what you're supposed to get? How much money do you have?"

Sandra hadn't thought about paying for the fish. Pulling two loonies from her pocket, she said, "Just my allowance."

The woman laughed loudly. "You'll need more than that to buy something in here. Whatever gave you that idea? Run along now, dear," she said, turning to another customer.

Feeling her face flush, Sandra shuffled around the corner of the lobster tank. She had turned the wrong way. Instead of heading back outside, she was now facing toward the back of the store. Not wanting to go past the woman again, she stepped toward a clerk who was working behind a low steel counter.

The counter top held trays of cut-up fish. As the man flipped another fillet onto one of the trays, he noticed Sandra and winked. Tufts of grey-flecked hair curled out from under a green toque on his head. With the back of his hand, the man nudged his wire-framed glasses back in place. Then he bent his head and continued with his work.

Sandra walked closer and peered behind the counter. With rapid strokes of his knife, the man was slicing up fish. The head and the tail, the bones, and the insides of each fish he pushed into a plastic garbage pail.

Taking a big breath, Sandra spoke to the man.

"Are you throwing that stuff out?"

The man straightened, and pushed his shoulders back to stretch. With one finger he scratched

under his toque. Laying the knife on the table, he wiped his hands on his yellow apron. "Yeah," he said, "I'm throwing this out. Why?"

"I need some," Sandra answered.

"You can't eat this stuff, you know. This is what you eat," he said, pointing to the counter top.

"I know. It's... it's... " Sandra hesitated. "It's for my pet."

"Oh, you got a little guy that likes fish, eh? Okay." The man reached for a white plastic bag lying in a pile at the end of the counter. Picking up the garbage pail, he shook fish scraps into the bag until the bottom bulged out.

"That enough?" he asked.

"Yes, thanks."

The man twirled the bag and fastened the top with a plastic tie. As he held the bag over the counter, he wiggled his fingers. Sandra stared. Half of his second finger was missing.

"Too bad about that," he said, twisting his hand around. "Sometimes I'm just too fast for my own good. I was cutting fish one day and scraping the guts into this pail and I looked down and noticed half my finger was gone. Ended up with the fish guts, I guess. Never did find it."

Yuck, Sandra thought, as she wrinkled her face in disgust. When the man held the bag closer to her, Sandra glanced at his face. He winked.

Sandra grabbed the bag and walked quickly to the door.

Chapter 8

The sky was still thick with falling snow. Headlights from passing cars shone dimly in the grey light.

When she reached the riverbank, Sandra cupped her hands around her eyes and peered into the blizzard. She could see dark green water spilling over the weir, tumbling into the waves at the bottom of the waterfall. She couldn't see the pelican.

Sandra looked carefully along the falls to the far side of the river. There something white floated on the black water rushing under the ice.

"Oh, Pelly!" Sandra cried. "Why couldn't you be on this side of the river? Now what am I supposed to do with this stupid fish?"

Sandra turned and walked slowly away from the river. Soon she found herself at the bottom of a set of steep wooden stairs.

The steps were filled with snow. With one hand

on the railing and the other clutching the bag of fish, Sandra kicked toeholds into the drifts. All the way to the top her eyes were locked on the steps just ahead. When there were no more stairs to climb, she took a big breath and looked around.

She was where she had never been before – on top of the hill that led to the railway bridge.

Everything, on all sides, above and below, was swirling snow. The railway tracks, two long ridges in the snow, stretched into the white space above the river.

Sandra stepped quickly to the bridge walkway that ran beside the tracks. Looking straight ahead, she grabbed the railing and started across.

Before long, she stopped. The walkway was visible for just a few steps in front of her and a few steps behind. Except for the soft hum coming from the falls somewhere below her, Sandra might have been on any city sidewalk.

She quickened her pace. Her hand became a little snowplough that shot a stream of snow off the top of the railing.

At the other end of the bridge, a short set of stairs led down to the top of the steep riverbank. When Sandra looked over the edge of the bank, she saw clumps of skinny branches pushing out of the snow. She stumbled and slid down the hill and stepped over the fallen wires of a fence almost buried in the snow.

On hands and knees, dragging the bag of fish, she crawled over ice-covered rocks until she reached the edge of the heaving water. The roar of the falls made her body quake. It seemed like the rocks themselves were vibrating and might shake her into the river.

Her heart racing in fear, Sandra backed away from the water. Mist from the falls fell over her face like icy water from a spray bottle. Sandra wiped her sleeve across her cheeks and forehead.

A few metres from shore Pelly bobbed in the water. "Pelly!" Sandra yelled. The pelican raised her head and paddled toward the girl.

"You must be starving, Pelly! Look what I brought you."

After tugging off her mitts, Sandra peeled scraps of fish from the cold slush inside the bag. Lifting her arm over her shoulder, she threw the bits to the waiting pelican. Pelly quickly grabbed each piece.

Sandra stuffed the empty plastic bag into her jacket pocket. Her hands ached from the cold and wet.

"I have to go, Pelly," Sandra said. "I'll catch it if I'm not home when Dad gets there."

As Sandra turned to go, the pelican seemed to shiver from her chest to the tip of her bill.

Chapter 9

When Sandra returned to the fish store the next day, the man knew what she wanted.

"You back again?" he asked, reaching for a plastic bag. "You must have one hungry tom at your place. Or are you feeding a whole family?"

"No, just one," Sandra answered.

"Must be a big guy," the man laughed.

"I guess so," Sandra said, thinking of Pelly's long neck and broad wings.

"I've got a couple of them at home, too," the man said. "They go crazy over this fish." He pushed his glasses further up on his nose. "One time I was feeding them some fish right from my hand. They started fighting over it. Well, one wanted it so bad he jumped in and took a wild bite.."

As if he had just cut himself, the man jerked his hand up and shook it. He held his hand over the

counter to show the finger cut off halfway down.

"He got everything, too. The whole fish, and my finger. Don't ever feed them fish right from your hand, eh." The man grinned.

Sandra couldn't think of anything to say. The man's story couldn't be true. It was the same finger he'd told her about the day before.

"Here you go," the man said, holding a bag of fish scraps across the counter top. "That should keep him for a while!"

"Thank you," Sandra said, already turning to leave.

When she got to the river, Pelly was still on the far side. Remembering her trip in the blizzard, Sandra went right to the bridge and started across. This time she had a clear view from the walkway. In the distance she could see what looked like black paint spilled along the edge of the river ice. It was a channel of open water that flowed around a curve in the river and stopped a few hundred metres from the weir. Sandra wandered why that water wasn't frozen.

Below her, at the waterfall, Sandra saw that Pelly had been joined by a small flock of ducks. As they jostled around the pelican, the ducks dipped their heads underwater and stuck their rumps in the air. It looked to Sandra as if Pelly was nudging the smaller birds with her long bill, the way a big dog might nuzzle a kitten.

By the time Sandra slid down the hill to the shore, the ducks had flown away.

Chapter 10

On the day before Christmas, Wesley came home from work at lunch time. He found Sandra watching television. Somehow the few gifts lying under the tree made the apartment look barer than usual.

"I'm going to go load up with a few groceries, and do some other stuff," he said. "I'll be back in a couple of hours." He bent down to ruffle Sandra's hair. "It's a good day for you to just lie around, kid. It must be about thirty below outside."

When Sandra didn't answer, Wesley went on. "Might even be a surprise. Maybe a parcel or something from Grandma Betty on the bus."

Sandra rolled over and looked up at her dad. "I wish," she said. "It's going to be pretty boring around here, that's for sure."

"Well, don't go anywhere," Wesley smiled. "You might miss something!"

"Yeah, right."

When Sandra heard her dad's car leave the parking lot, she pulled on her warm winter clothing. Outside, the freezing air stung the inside of her nose. The snow crackled under her boots. Holding one mitt over her face, Sandra walked quickly to the fish store.

The shop was crowded with customers. Sandra joined a line in front of the man's counter. Soon she was hot and sweaty under her heavy clothing. It seemed to be hours until it was her turn.

"There's lots of stuff for you today, cat lover!" the man greeted her. "How about two bags? We're going to be closed for a few days."

Looking up from his table, the man winked and motioned with his head for Sandra to move closer. "Come around the end here," he said. "This place is too noisy to carry on a conversation."

When Sandra was behind the counter, he asked, "What's your name, anyway? I like to call my best customers by name."

"Sandra."

"Good," he said. "And my name's Ernie. Think this'll be good enough? he asked, holding up two bags.

"I think so."

"Say, are you sure this is all for one pet?"

"Sort of." Sandra shrugged.

"Well, it makes no difference to me. It'll all be thrown out anyway." The man smiled at Sandra. "Sure is cold out, eh? You know, one time I was out ice fishing on a day like today. You ever been ice fishing?" he asked.

As the man pulled his toque further over his forehead, Sandra nodded.

"Well, one time I was out ice fishing and it was so cold we could hardly keep the hole open. But we didn't want to stop, because the fish were really biting.

"Every minute or so we'd have to chop more ice out of the hole, it would freeze that fast. It just got colder and colder and the ice formed faster and faster. Finally, I'd had enough. I started to pull in my line. But just before the end of the line came out of the hole, a fish bit into the hook.

"Well, I hauled up the line with one hand, and grabbed for the fish with the other." The man reached one hand then the other over the table. "Right when I got my hand on the fish, the hole froze over – like that!" The man snapped his fingers.

"There I was, my line, the fish, and my hand all stuck in the ice. Without thinking I just pulled as hard as I could." He jerked one hand above his head. "And I got my line, and the fish, but," he let his hand drop down in front of Sandra, "part of my finger stayed in the ice." Sandra stared at the stub of a finger on the man's left hand. Did he really expect her to believe that? It was as nutty as his other stories.

Now that he had finished, it seemed Ernie didn't know what else to say. He straightened some fillets in a tray on the counter top.

"I guess I should go," Sandra said, and gave the man a little smile. "Thanks for this stuff."

"Oh sure, any time. And have a good Christmas, you and your cat!"

Chapter 11

About halfway across the bridge, the children stopped running and looked over the railing.

"I told you," one boy said, pointing to the water near the falls, "It's that same pelican. It never left. I found a path, too." The boy led the other two along the trail Sandra had tramped into the riverbank snowdrifts.

With her bill dragging in the water, Pelly swam close to shore. Stepping over the broken fence, the children huddled together and shouted above the noise of the falls.

"It must be almost dead," the girl said.

The boy who had led the way there answered. "Yeah, it should be easy to catch this time. I'm going to get it to come closer so I can grab it." Crouching down, he slid one foot after the other across the top of the slippery rocks. Nearing the edge of the fast-flowing, black water, he stopped. "Geez, I don't know," he said, "this is pretty dangerous. I don't want to fall in." He slowly backed away from the water.

"Maybe we should leave it," the girl said. "Just let it go."

"Let it go?" the redhead snorted. "Are you guys chicken, or what? Here, I'll do it." Pushing past the other boy, he held out one arm behind his back. "Hold on to me," he said.

When his friends gripped his wrist, the boy knelt down and called to the pelican. "Come on, come here, I've got something for you." He shook his hand over the water and Pelly paddled closer. Just out of his reach, the pelican stopped. The redhead leaned out further.

"Hey, watch out," the other boy warned. "You could slip."

"Just wait. I can almost touch it."

The pelican lifted her bill out of the water. The redhead grabbed and missed. As his friends pulled him backward he slipped on the icy rocks and fell. One foot caught beneath him, and the other splashed into the frigid water.

With a startled cry, the redhead yanked his foot from the river. "Stupid bird!" he yelled. "That water's freezing!" Still sitting, he pushed himself back beside his friends. "Let's get it." Turning, he looked at the snowbank behind them. The mist from the falls had formed a hard crust on the snow. "Come on," the boy said. With his dry foot, he kicked frozen chunks from the snowbank. The other two children stood watching him. "Come on!" he called, and tossed each of them a piece of ice.

"Now, you stupid bird, you're really going to get

it!" he cried. Taking aim, the boy threw the chunk at Pelly. The sharp piece of ice struck the pelican at the base of her neck. Arching her wings, she hopped backwards in the water.

"Come on, you guys," the redhead shouted, "throw something at it."

Another piece hit Pelly as she twisted around. The pelican flapped her wings and skimmed across the narrow strip of water.

With all his might, the redhead threw one last chunk of ice. It splashed harmlessly into the waves below the falls. "Aw, great," he grumbled. "Now we'll never get it. A lot of help you guys were."

Before the redhead turned around, the girl dropped the ice chunk from her hand.

"I found it, remember," the other boy said. "Anyway, it has to stay around here. There's no place else for it to go, right? All we have to do is wait for it to come back."

"Well, I'm not waiting for it," the redhead said. "My foot's frozen stiff. I have to get home."

Close to the other shore, Pelly turned to fly above the falls. Higher and higher she climbed. Then, soaring with the air currents, she flew away from the weir, following the band of black water hugging the shore of the river.

As the three children scrambled up the riverbank, Sandra was leaving the warmth of the fish store. And a few blocks away, in the bus station, Wesley was getting ready to pick up Sandra's surprise.

Chapter 12

Sandra's grandmother was the last person off the bus from Big River. On the bottom step, she stopped and pulled a hood over her head. The reddish brown fur trim matched her short curly hair. She peered over the heads of passengers looking for luggage beside the bus. When she spotted Wesley inside the bus station, she smiled and waved.

"Is this all the welcome I get?" she asked as Wesley kissed her on the cheek. "I mean, it's nice to see you, but where's my little girl?"

Wesley laughed. "She's at home," he said. "I never told her you were coming. And I don't think she's guessed. so you're her surprise Christmas present."

"How's she been doing lately?" Grandma Betty asked. "Is she pretty lonely down here?"

"Some of the time. I know she's not too happy

about staying here for Christmas. She still misses Big River. And you, of course. But when I got a chance at a paying job, even just for a couple of weeks, I couldn't pass it up."

"Every little bit helps," Grandma Betty agreed. "That box over there is my bit of help. There must be enough baking in there to last a month!"

"All right! I was hoping you'd bring something, but I was afraid to ask. Wait here, Mom. I'll go get the box and your suitcase."

While Wesley walked outside to the bus, Sandra's grandmother looked around the station. The air was hazy with cigarette smoke. Beside her, a line of people curled toward a door leading to another bus. As the driver punched tickets, children and adults shuffled slowly forward, nudging suitcases and bags.

Wesley came up behind his mother and touched her lightly on the elbow.

"I'm just thinking," she said. "It doesn't look very festive around here. Everybody looks so sad. Maybe they're just worried about not getting home in time for Christmas."

"Maybe," Wesley said. "I'm glad you got here okay. It's going to be good, having us all together for the holidays." He started toward the door of the bus station. "I can't wait to see Sandra's face when you walk in the door!"

Chapter 13

Sandra was leaning against the railing at the top of the stairs to the railway bridge. Puffs of breath formed little clouds around her head. The scarf covering her mouth was white with ice crystals.

As soon as she started across the walkway, Sandra sensed something was wrong. Without stopping, she turned to look down at the strip of water by the falls. The pelican wasn't there. Sandra walked faster. Then, with the bags bouncing against her legs, she began to run.

Every few seconds she slowed down to look over the railing. Maybe, she thought, Pelly was just hidden by a pile of ice. Maybe when I look this time, I'll see her paddling in the water again.

When she reached the end of the bridge, Sandra stopped to catch her breath. Holding the bags tightly in her hands, she slid down the path to the waterfall. For a few moments she stood still, searching all along the edge of the water. The bags dropped from her hands and she slumped onto the rocks.

Sandra wrapped her arms around her knees and pulled her legs against her chest. She stared across the water. She was sure Pelly hadn't died and been swept under the ice. The pelican had been getting stronger. so why, she wondered, would Pelly leave now?

Cold was seeping through the seat of Sandra's pants. As she stood up she saw that the snow around her was trampled with many footprints. The snowbank behind her was flattened. Someone had been there and scared Pelly away!

If Pelly had been frightened, Sandra told herself, she might come back when it was safe. Picking up the bags, Sandra dumped the fish pieces onto the ground. Some of the chunks she threw on the ice below the falls. Others she just kicked off the rocks into the river.

Icy slush from the fish and soaked into Sandra's mitts. She tugged off each mitt and pushed it into a jacket pocket. After squishing the bags into a pock-et, she wriggled her hands, now stinging from the cold, into her sleeves.

Chapter 14

Sandra pushed open the door to her apartment building with her shoulder. At the bottom of the stairs she stopped, out of breath from running and from the cold that shook her body. By the time she reached her apartment, needles pricked her warming fingertips. Leaning against the door, she heard a familiar voice.

"Grandma!" she cried, turning the door knob.

Sandra's grandmother jumped, almost spilling hot tea onto the kitchen table. Moments later Sandra threw her arms around her grandmother's neck.

"Whoa!" Grandma Betty laughed, "now that's the kind of welcome I like! Here, let me take a look at you. I think you've grown a bunch since I last saw you."

"Maybe," Sandra said. Pulling away, she looked up into her grandmother's face. "You got your hair done. I like it."

"Thank you! I thought I could use a little colour for Christmas."

"Are you staying with us for Christmas, Grandma?" Sandra asked excitedly. "Really?"

"I heard your tree looked pretty empty. So I thought I'd be like Santa Claus and bring some presents down from the north. Say, where've you been that you weren't home when I got here?" Grandma Betty sniffed. "And what's that smell?" She caught Sandra's hand and sniffed again. "Smells like fish. And your hands are freezing! What've you been up to?"

"It's kind of a long story, Grandma," Sandra said, looking down at the floor.

"Then we'd better all hear it!" Wesley spoke suddenly from behind them.

Sandra looked up, "Hi, Dad," she murmured. "Have you been home long?"

"Long enough to wonder where you'd gotten to," he said angrily. "What's this story you've got to tell? It doesn't have anything to do with a pelican, does it?"

"Yes."

"Geez," Wesley shook his head. "I thought you got that out of your system months ago."

Coming around the corner with the teapot and three cups, Grandma Betty nudged past Sandra into the living room. "This is starting to sound interesting," she said. "You hang up your stuff, Sandra. Then we'll all get comfy and you can tell us your long story."

"Sandra," Wesley said, "I told you months ago you were not to go down to the river. And today you weren't even supposed to leave the apartment." Pointing his finger at Sandra, he said, "You are in big trouble."

"I was just trying to keep her alive!" Sandra cried. "What's so bad about that?"

Before Wesley could answer, Grandma Betty spoke. "Come, Sandra," she said. "You're still shivering. Have some tea. Wrap yourself up in a blanket. And Wesley, hold on a minute. Let Sandra warm up and tell us her story."

Sandra sat cross-legged on the couch and wrapped a blanket over her shoulders. "When we first moved here," she said quietly, "I found the pelicans down by the waterfall." She took a sip of the tea that Grandma Betty had loaded with lots of sugar and milk. After a quick glance at her grandmother, Sandra continued. By the time she had finished talking the teapot was empty.

"Well, that's something," Grandma Betty said. "And after all that, you think the pelican's been driven off somewhere?"

"So now we'll never see it, right?" Wesley spoke sharply. "That's been the problem all along." He turned to Grandma Betty. "She says she's had this pelican friend since we moved here. but no-one else has ever seen it. I've even gone down to the river with her a few times. No pelican ever came up to her like she says it did."

Looking back at Sandra, he added, "And now you say it's flown off, so again we don't know if it's really true."

"It is true!" Sandra cried. "It all really happened just like I said. I can't help it if Pelly only comes for me. I'm not lying!"

Tears fell from Sandra's eyes as she flung herself across the couch. Grandma Betty reached over to rub her back.

"Hey, Sandra," she said softly, "no-one's saying you're lying. Your daddy just means he has to see it with his own eyes before he believes it. And me? I'll believe you if you say it's so."

Grandma Betty continued. "But I don't think there's much we can do about it today. How be we leave it until after Christmas? Would that be all right? If the pelican has flown away, you can't do anything more for it anyway."

"She won't be doing anything more for it, period." Wesley said. "You're grounded, Sandra. From now on, you can't go anywhere without me. That's one of the stupidest things I ever heard of. To get fish from some store and then tramp down to the

54

river to feed some make-believe bird. If something had happened, I never would have found you."

"She's not make-believe," Sandra argued, pulling fluff from the couch. "And nothing happened."

"Okay, you two, okay," Grandma Betty said. "Listen, Sandra, you probably should have told your father where you were going. But she's right, Wesley, nothing bad happened to her. So, let's forget it for now. It's almost Christmas, remember?"

Grandma Betty pushed herself off the couch. "You two wait here. I'm going to get my Santa's bag from the bedroom."

Chapter 15

On the day after Boxing Day, Sandra and her grandmother were hunched over a card table in the living-room. Using a small wooden tool with a metal hook at one end, Sandra pulled a short piece of yarn through a hole in a jute mat. Grandma Betty wore her reading glasses as she cut more lengths of yarn. The different coloured pieces she pushed into separate piles along the edge of the table.

The rug-hooking kit was one of Sandra's presents. Grandma Betty had designed a picture of a loon swimming on a lake.

"Look how much we've got done," Sandra called to Wesley, who was lying on the couch. She leaned back on her chair, lifted the rug off the table, and turned to look at her father. "This is the head. Can you tell?"

"You bet," Wesley answered, "it looks great."

"It'll be really nice when its finished," Sandra said. "I'm going to put it on the wall in my room."

"Don't lean back on your chair like that," Grandma Betty said quietly. "You might wreck it."

Sandra sat forward and laid the rug on the table. She slid her hands lightly along the arms of the chair. The light-coloured wood had been sanded as smooth as driftwood, without a scratch or dent.

"This is such a beautiful chair, Daddy," Sandra said. "I can't believe you hid it at Jason's and I never saw it. Did it take you a long time to make?"

"Not too long." Wesley smoothed his moustache. "It was one of the projects for my course, so I could work at it every day."

As Wesley picked up his newspaper, Sandra reached for another piece of yarn. The room was silent until Grandma Betty asked, "So, where's this place you get the fish?"

Sandra and her father looked at each other. "Well," Grandma Betty said, taking off her glasses, "I like a good fish supper. I thought maybe we could go there and get a few fillets."

Smiling at her grandmother, Sandra asked, "And maybe get some fish scraps for you know who?"

"Sure, we could do that," Grandma Betty turned in her chair. "What do you say, Wesley?"

"Uh, maybe count me out," he answered, snapping the newspaper above his chest.

"Oh, come on," Grandma Betty insisted. "Why don't you drive us to this fish place. You don't have to come in. Sandra and I'll get some stuff, and then you can drive us to the river. We'll see if we can find this pelican. That way we'll know for sure, right?"

With a grunt Wesley agreed.

A short time later Sandra and her grandmother

were in the seafood store. There were only a few customers. Taking Grandma Betty's hand, Sandra led the way to Ernie's counter.

"Hi there, Sandra!" he said. "Back for more, eh? I see you brought someone to help carry the fish."

"This is my Grandma Betty," Sandra answered. "Grandma, this is Ernie. We want some fillets, and some other stuff."

"It must be quite a cat this girl's feeding," Ernie said.

Feeling her grandmother looking at her, Sandra said, "Actually, I don't really have a cat." As Ernie leaned closer, she went on. "I just let you think I had one, so you'd give me the fish scraps. I've been using the stuff to feed a pelican at the river."

Ernie tugged at his toque. "A pelican?" he asked.

"She stayed at the waterfall when all the other pelicans left because I fed her popcorn," Sandra explained. "And now she can't find any food in the river, because it's too cold. So I have to take her fish scraps to eat."

"Is that right?" Ernie said. "I didn't know pelicans stayed here all winter." He glanced at Sandra, then over at her grandmother.

"They're grand birds, pelicans," he said. "I like to watch them down on the river, too. You know, I've never seen them fighting. Not with each other or with any other birds. They're always calm and quiet."

Ernie put his hands on the counter top. Shaking his head, he leaned toward Sandra. "Not like geese," he said. "You ever have anything to do with geese, Sandra? No? Well, they're just mean and noisy, those birds.

"I remember once when I was a kid, I visited a

farm that had geese. The guy told me I could feed them. Well, I didn't know any better, so I got right in the pen with them, with this pail of feed.

"They were honking and squawking all around me, trying to get at the feed. Before I could pour it out, they knocked the pail right out of my hand! Most of the feed spilled on the ground, and all the geese charged at it.

"I was scared by then, with these geese fighting all around me. I wanted to get out, but I figured I'd better get the pail back. So I reached down to get the pail, and just then a big gander turned around and tried to bite my hand.

"He got a bit of it, all right." Ernie held up the hand with one finger half gone. "And I took off and left the pail right where it was."

Ernie looked down at Sandra and pushed up his glasses. "What do you think of that?"

"I think that's a crazy story!" Sandra laughed. "I thought it was a cat that bit off your finger, or the ice."

Ernie shrugged.

"Oh, he has lots of stories about his missing finger," Sandra explained. "I don't think any of them are true."

Laughing, Ernie asked, "So, you want some fillets today, too? How about whitefish? That's what you've been feeding the pelican."

When Grandma Betty nodded, Ernie went on, "I don't know how a pelican could ever stay alive in this cold, though."

Sandra frowned. "I don't know if she is any more. The last time I went to the falls, she was gone. I think she got scared off. We're going to look for her now."

"Well, let me know if you find it, okay? And if you need more fish scraps, there's always lots here."

Wesley never spoke when they got back in the car. During the ride to the river, the only talking came from the car radio.

Even before they started up the steps to the walkway, Sandra knew Pelly wasn't at the waterfall. In the middle of the bridge, they stopped. Sandra pointed to the water at the far end of the weir.

"That's where I fed her the fish," she said. "She seemed to like it more on that side of the river. I think she thought it was safe over there."

"It would be by itself, all right," Grandma Betty agreed. "But you said the last time you went down there someone else had been around."

"There were lots of footprints. And I don't know why else she would leave."

Leaning against the railing, Wesley studied the strip of water below the falls and stayed silent.

"Look at that bit of water above the weir," Grandma Betty said. "That's strange. Why wouldn't the water up there be frozen like it is everywhere else?"

Wesley looked up. "That's water from the power plant. They take in river water and heat it up when they're making electricity. When the water goes back into the river, it's warm enough that it doesn't freeze right away. That's the power plant over there. We can just see the smokestacks over the buildings downtown."

"So there's warm water up there," Grandma Betty said. "Did you know that, Sandra?"

"I knew some of the water wasn't frozen," Sandra said. "But I didn't know why."

"Do you think your bird would be smart enoug
to find open water?"

"I don't know. Maybe."

"I guess we'd better find out," Grandma Betty
said. "Why don't you drive us there, Wesley?"

Sandra's father sighed. "It'd be a waste of time.
Look at this river. It's solid ice. One little bit of
water isn't going to make any difference. Besides,
the weather's been below zero for over a month.
There's no way a pelican could live here all winter."
He turned to Sandra. "I don't know what you
thought you saw down here. But it sure wasn't a
pelican."

"Now, Wesley," Grandma Betty said, "let's check
everything out before we decide there isn't any pelican. Is it hard to get there? No? Let's go then.
Come Sandra."

Wesley laughed and shook his head. "This is
becoming too much of a wild goose chase."

As she started down the steps, Sandra wasn't
sure she wanted to go to the power plant, either. If
Pelly wasn't there, it could mean only one thing.

Chapter 16

The channel of open water that could be seen from the bridge was only a few metres wide. A kilometre up the river, near the power plant, the channel was almost a hundred metres across. It was here that warm water from the plant entered the river through an underground pipe. At the beginning of the open water, a small building stood on a concrete pad a little ways out from the shore.

Sandra, Wesley, and Grandma Betty walked from the car along a path that followed the top of the riverbank. Grandma Betty carried the bag of fish scraps. First to see the birds was Wesley.

"Ducks!" he said. "By the building there, must be a dozen of them. Now, that's something, I didn't know they could stay over winter. That water's warm enough for them, I guess."

As she looked quickly at the ducks, and then away, Sandra chewed on her lip. Something terrible had happened to Pelly. "She's not here," she sa. quietly.

"No, Sandra," Wesley said, "there's no pelican here."

Grandma Betty was staring hard at the little building in the river. "You know," she said, "there's something about white animals surrounded by ice. It makes them really hard to spot."

"What do you mean Grandma?" Sandra asked.

"Well," Grandma Betty answered, "there's something on the other side of that building. Maybe it's just a piece of ice. but it keeps coming out around the corner, then popping back again. You watch, Sandra."

As Sandra looked down at the river, a large white bird floated backwards from behind the building. When it was almost all in view, it paddled back out of sight.

"That's Pelly!" Sandra cried.

"Geez," Wesley shook his head. "There really is a pelican."

"Where's the fish stuff?" Sandra asked. Grabbing the bag, Sandra stepped off the path toward the top of the river bank.

"Hey!" Wesley called, "Where do you think you're going?"

Turning back to her father, Sandra said, "I have to get this food to her. She must be starving."

"No way. It's too steep down there. You'd probably fall in."

"Daddy, she needs this food! She's waiting for me to feed her."

Wesley glanced at the pelican, which was now paddling in one spot beside the little building. Then he looked at the riverbank below him.

ere, give me the bag," he said. "We'll make a
n down together."

Sandra and Wesley worked their way down to
he shoreline about thirty metres from the building.
Sandra took the bag and dumped the fish onto the
snow. She called Pelly's name. then she looked over
at her father. "She might not come if you're here.
could you go back with Grandma?

"Okay," he said. "But don't go any closer to the
water than this."

As her father climbed up the hill, Sandra called
again to the pelican. Pelly drifted out from behind
the building and swam right to Sandra.

From the path, Wesley and Grandma Betty
watched Sandra toss pieces of fish to the pelican.
The bird calmly scooped up each scrap. Sandra
crouched down and said something to the pelican.
As if listening carefully, the bird stared at her. Then
Sandra stood up on tiptoe and stretched out her
arms. Arching out of the water, the pelican spread
her wings.

"I don't think I believe this," Wesley muttered. "I
guess she really has been feeding that pelican."

Grandma Betty chuckled. "I guess she has. You

know, that's quite a girl you've got there."

When Sandra climbed back up to the pathway, she was beaming. "Did you see her?" she asked.

"Did we ever!" Wesley said. He grabbed Sandra and gave her a tight hug. "I owe you a big apology, kid," he said. "I never believed you."

"I know," Sandra said. "That's why I never told you I was still coming to the river. I knew you wouldn't believe me until you saw her for yourself. And now you finally got to see her." Turning to her grandmother, Sandra asked, "Isn't she beautiful?"

"She is lovely, Sandra," Grandma Betty said, "and she sure looked happy to see you!"

Sandra looked up at her father. "I want to keep feeding her. She really does need me to bring her stuff, Dad. The water's too cold for her to get fish on her own."

Frowning, Wesley turned back toward the car. Sandra and her grandmother followed. As she opened a back door, Sandra spoke up. "There'll be lots of scraps for her at the fish store. Ernie will keep saving them for me. I just have to pick up the stuff and bring it down here. It won't take long."

Wesley started the motor. "What I said before Christmas still goes, Sandra. You can't come down here by yourself."

"You could bring me," Sandra said, leaning over the back of the front seat.

"No, I don't have time to drive down here every day."

"It doesn't have to be every day. Just once a week. Okay? Once a week."

"Well, we'll see," Wesley said.

Grandma Betty shifted in the front seat, enough to look back at Sandra, and winked.

Chapter 17

Sandra answered the knock on her apartment door to find Jason and Robert.

"He really did it this time!" Jason blurted.

"Who?" Sandra asked.

"No Pets," Robert said, looking worried. "He's stuck in a tree."

"He's way up in that big tree down the block," Jason said, "and he won't come down."

"Why did he climb up there?"

"Who knows," Jason snorted. "We've been calling him for half an hour, and he won't even look at us."

"Jason even threw sticks at him," Robert said, "but he just sits there."

"He's close enough that you can throw stuff at him?" Sandra asked.

"Oh yeah," Jason said, "I almost hit him, but he's not smart enough to be scared. What a bird brain!"

"Wait here," Sandra said. "Maybe I've got something that'll get him down."

When Sandra came back a few minutes later, she was carrying a white plastic bag. She kept the top twisted around her wrist until they reached the tree.

"What's in there?" Robert asked.

Sandra opened the bag. She dumped onto the ground a fish head and some small, bony fillets.

"Gross!" Robert made a face.

"Where'd you get that?" his brother asked.

"From a friend of ours," Sandra said. "Here," she handed Jason the frozen fish head, "throw this up near No Pets."

Jason held the head lightly in his hand. Then he heaved it up into the tree. It struck a branch and fell back to the ground. After a few more tries, the fish sailed close to No Pets. Sniffing cautiously, the cat crept a ways down the branch.

"He's moving!" Robert said.

Slowly, with many throws, the cat was drawn down the tree. As each piece of fish broke apart, it was left on the ground near the bottom of the tree. When No Pets reached the last big branch, he stopped to stare at the scraps of fish. He was still about two metres from the ground. "Mmrrup!" he called as he swished his tail.

"No-oo," Jason cried. "Don't jump!"

No Pets was in the air, his feet stuck out in front and behind. Straight down he dropped, plunging almost out of sight into a snow bank. He lay motionless as Sandra knelt to pick him up. Draped over her shoulder and petted softly, he began to purr.

After a few moments, the cat twisted his head around to look down at the ground. As he twitched his whiskers, Sandra spread him on the snow

ide some fish. One paw reached out and pulled
e scrap over to his mouth. No Pets slipped onto
his haunches and with loud smacking bites began
chewing the fish.

Near the shore by the power plant, Pelly was being
tempted with bits of fish, too. A man had climbed
down to the ridge of rocks close to the little building.

"Hey, pelican, I've got something for you," he
called softly.

The man dropped some fish pieces into the
water. With her bill resting against the front of her
neck, Pelly stared at the man. She made no sign of
moving.

"Aw, you're right to be shy," he said. "Here, I'll
make it easier." The rest of the fish he threw closer
to the pelican.

After reaching into his parka hood to push up
his glasses, the man climbed to the top of the hill.
There he stood to watch the pelican. Pelly swam
away from the side of the building and scooped up
a piece of fish. Quickly she grabbed another and
another.

"Yeah!" the man said each time Pelly's head
jerked up to swallow a scrap of fish. "You like that
stuff, eh? I can get lots of it. You know bird, if
you're going to make it through the winter, you're
going to need more than what Sandra can bring
you. Maybe I'll come by once or twice a week
myself. I don't think I'll tell Sandra, though. This'll
be our little secret."

Chapter 18

One mild afternoon in March, heavy, wet snowflakes began to settle on Saskatoon. Through the night, the snow fell. The next morning, as the temperature dropped, the slush on the roads froze into ruts. A slippery crust covered the new snow banks.

It was about noon when a voice called to Polly. The pelican paddled quickly away from her shelter. The shore was empty.

"I'm up here, pelican!" the man shouted from the top of the bank. "I had to walk halfway here because the roads are blocked. I don't have time to make a new path down to you. But I've got some stuff." He turned upside down the bag he was carrying and dumped fish scraps onto the snow.

Grabbing the pieces a handful at a time, he heaved them over the riverbank. Some pieces splashed into the water near the shore. Many land-n the snow-covered rocks at the river's edge.

"That should keep you, pelican," the man said. .e waved and walked away.

A short time later, a large dog trotted up to the riverbank. It was a skinny creature, with thick brown fur and dark brown pads on its paws. In the summer, this dog ate small animals, like gophers and newly hatched birds. All winter it had lived on what it could drag from garbage cans. It was always hungry.

The dog sniffed the snow where the fish had been dumped first. As it chewed up the few little bits the man had missed, a low growl came from its throat.

Pelly paddled near the shore and swallowed the scraps floating in the water. More of her food lay in the snow, just out of reach.

Keeping her head turned toward the bank, the pelican drifted along the rocky shoreline. She stopped where the snow sloped right down to the river. Trying to clamber onto the stones beneath the snow, she fell back into the water. She tried again and once more slipped from an icy rock.

Finally, she heaved herself onto the snowbank and stood upright on her wobbly legs. She bent her head and began picking up the fish scraps.

On the riverbank above, the dog stiffened and stood still. Its ears had picked up a slight noise, a noise that could lead it to prey. Slinking low to the ground, it padded softly toward the edge of the riverbank. Not able to see all the way to the shoreline, the dog began to pick its way down the snow-covered slope.

When she had swallowed all the fish she could reach, Pelly spread her wings and hopped to another rock. With her long bill, she picked up two more scraps. She swung her head to look at the ducks feeding near the power plant. Then she turned back and hopped further along the shoreline.

The dog steadied itself on a ridge of snow. From below came flashes of white head feathers, yellow beak and black wingtips. The dog's body twitched with tension. One front paw slipped through the snow. It pulled back quickly and braced itself to leap over the ridge.

As Pelly bent her head to pick up another piece of fish, a trickle of snow rolled down the bank to her foot. In one slow movement, the pelican swung her head to look from the bottom of the bank to the top.

With a vicious snarl, the dog jumped. Arching her wings, the pelican sprang toward the water. As the dog landed, its jaws snapped shut. The nails on its front feet raked over the snow. One paw snagged Pelly's wing tip.

The pelican was jerked from the air. With one

flapping, she fell into the shallow water near
the shore. She twisted her head to stare at the dog.
Snarling, the dog shuffled its three free paws to get
a better footing on the rocks. Pelly tugged her wing,
but it was held fast. She tugged again. The wing
didn't move. She was trapped.

The dog shifted more weight to its back legs. The
pelican's body was less than two metres away.
Pulling its front paw back sharply on Pelly's wing,
the dog lunged at the bird's breast.

In the instant that the dog was in the air, Pelly
jerked her wing. It came free. She beat her wings
and pushed off from the shore.

When the dog landed, one front paw glanced off
the side of an icy rock. Scrambling to find a grip, it
was thrown off balance. It's jaw cracked into the
rock. The other front paw swung wildly.

Pelly was out of reach. With ragged wingbeats,
she skipped across the water toward the power
plant.

The dog snuffled the feathers stuck to its paw
and barked at the pelican. It barked again, then
turned to snatch the piece of fish Pelly had left
behind. Quickly it sniffed out the other fish scraps.
When it had tramped all along the shoreline, the
dog scrambled up the bank and trotted away.

Chapter 19

With a loud crack, a huge chunk of ice fell into the river. It dropped almost out of sight, rose slowly to the surface and floated silently in the open water. Another piece broke away, then another. Soon the river was cluttered with icebergs.

Pelly swam into the midst of the floes. A wide, flat piece of ice, its top just above the water, drifted toward her. When the ice was close, Pelly arched her wings and jumped on.

As the iceberg carried her slowly down the river, Pelly preened herself. Standing on one leg, the pelican flicked her foot against her neck and head. She twisted and turned so she could clean the feathers on the underside of her wings and body.

Near the waterfall, some of the floes were bunching up against a sandbar. Surrounded suddenly by tall icebergs, Pelly was caught in the ice jam. She

...ldn't see past the walls of ice, and she couldn't ...retch her wings enough to fly over them. Pelly's ...aft shuddered. Grinding against the backed-up ice, it spun away from the sandbar and floated backwards up to the edge of the falls.

The waterfall is less than three metres high. It doesn't look dangerous, but it is. When the weir was built, a deep trench was scooped out of the bottom of the river, just below the falls. The water spilling over the weir drops through the air and then plunges right to the bottom of the trench.

Strange swirling currents are created below the waterfall. If a log or an animal is swept over the weir, it is dragged down to the bottom of the trench. When it finally pops up, it might be held in the churning water at the base of the falls for hours, or days, or months.

The pelican had no warning. One moment her ice raft was floating on the river, the next it was hurtling through the air.

Facing the waterfall, Pelly tried to push away from the falling raft. Her feet slipped. Whipping her wings back, Pelly slowed her fall. Again and again she beat her wings, but she couldn't lift herself over the top of the weir. More ice chunks vaulted over the falls, brushing against her wingtips.

The ragged ice below the falls leapt up to scrape against her feet. Her legs jerked up, but at the same time her body dropped a little closer to the thrashing water.

Pelly was tiring. Her wings beat more slowly. She drifted down. With a shock, her feet hit a block of ice that was tumbling away from the falls. As she pitched sideways, her wings thrashed in the air. She pushed hard against the ice.

And then, finally, she was away from the falls, skimming over the ice floes below the weir.

Quickly, Pelly climbed high above the river. With her neck doubled back and her legs tucked in, she glided with the air currents. She turned back toward the power plant. Following the course of the river, she zigzagged across it, beating her wings, coasting, turning.

When she reached the power plant, she dived down to the little building. Just above the water, she pushed back her wings and stuck out her legs. As the ducks paddled around her, Pelly nudged them with her bill.

Chapter 20

Under the clear sky, the river had turned a bright blue. Sunlight flickered like sparks along the top of the water.

Near the weir, a lone pelican was herding fish in the waves.

"Hi, Pelly!" Sandra shouted. "I've got your fish."

The pelican didn't stop feeding.

"Wait until she's finished eating," Sandra's father suggested, "then maybe she'll come closer."

A large shadow with outstretched wings floated across the surface of the river. A second pelican glided down to the falls.

"Which one do you think is Pelly?" Wesley asked. He swept a puddle of water from a park bench, then rubbed the seat with the sleeve of his jacket. "Well?" he asked again, laughing, as he sat down.

"The one –" Sandra started to point toward the waterfall. She stopped when she saw a small flock of ducks paddle out from behind some reeds near the shore. In the middle of the flock, stretching high above the brown bodies, swam a third white pelican.

"Pelly!"

Down the path Sandra dashed. When she was close to the birds, she pushed through a clump of willows and slid down the bank.

The ducks scattered when Sandra burst through the bushes, but the pelican stayed near the shore. Pulling her bill close to her neck, the bird stared at the girl. Sandra squatted in the mud by the water.

"Hi, Pelly." Taking a deep breath, Sandra tried to talk quietly. "Sorry I scared away your friends."

Sandra began to drop pieces of fish into the water. "You sure look pretty. All your freckles are gone! Even the yellow smudges on your front."

Warmed by the spring sun, Wesley watched from the bench. After a half-hour, he called to Sandra. She went up on tiptoe and spread her arms wide. The pelican arched her wings.

"See you," Sandra said. "Real soon, I hope."

"Didn't you give her all the fish?" Wesley asked, when Sandra reached him.

"No, I thought I'd save some."

"How come?"

"Well, I thought maybe I could come back again. By myself."

Wesley streatched his arms and took a deep breath. "It's pretty nice, all right. I guess you could come back by yourself. When were you thinking?"

"This afternoon."

Pushing himself up from the bench, Wesley put his arm on Sandra's shoulder. "You're not going to forget about your other friends, are you?" he asked. "Your human friends?"

No," Sandra laughed. "I'll still have lots of time play with those guys."

After lunch that day, Sandra found Jason and Robert digging ditches and building dams in the waterlogged alley behind the apartment building.

"Do you want to help?" Robert asked.

"No, not right now," Sandra shook her head.

Jason straightened up and leaned against his shovel. "What's in the bag?" he asked.

"Some stuff," Sandra answered, twirling the bag under her wrist. "Remember when we got No Pets out of the tree by throwing fish at him?"

"Yeah, that dummy!" Jason laughed.

"I've got more fish," Sandra said. "Do you want to see?" She opened the bag in front of Robert.

"Yuck! That gross stuff!" Robert cried. "What have you got that for?"

"I use it to feed a pelican at the river. I've been doing it all winter."

Jason shook his head. "No way. The river's been frozen up all winter."

"Not everywhere," Sandra said. "There was some warm water down by the power plant. That's where I used to feed her. Now she's over at the waterfall. I'm going back to see her right now."

"Yeah, right," Jason said. "There's probably lots of pelicans at the river by now. They come every year."

"No, not yet. Only three. And the other two just got there. But I can tell Pelly from the others."

"It even has a name?" Jason asked.

"Sure. And she comes to me when I call her."

"Uh-uh," Jason shook his head. "Those pelicans

78

never come near the shore."

"Pelly comes for me. You can see for yourself, you want."

"Come on, Jason," Robert said. "Let's go see."

Jason poked at a pile of mud with the blade of his shovel. "Okay," he said, "I guess there's lots of stuff to do down there, anyway."

When they got to the river, Sandra made the boys wait at the top of the bank. Shortly after Sanrda crouched on the shore, Pelly swam over. The pelican snatched the few pieces of fish that she dropped into the water.

"That was awesome!" Jason exclaimed when Sandra joined them on the riverbank.

"She came right to you, just like you said she would," Robert said. "And she waved to you when you left. Does she always do that? She's just like your pet!"

"Your pet!" Jason cried. "Hey, you could do your report on that pelican. That'd be great!" When Sandra frowned, Jason went on. "No, you should! Everyone else is telling about their boring cats and dogs. You'd be the only one with a pelican for a pet!"

"Aw, I don't know," Sandra said. "Everyone would laugh at me."

"Are you serious?" Jason asked. "They wouldn't. They'd be too jealous."

"Well, maybe," Sandra said. "Anyway. she's not really my pet. I've just been feeding her. And I won't even be doing that much longer."

"What do yo mean?" Robert asked.

"The rest of her flock will be here any day now. And then she'll go up north with them."

"How do you know?" Robert asked. "Why would

ave if you've been feeding her."

don't know for sure," Sandra said. "I guess I
st hope that's what she'll do. It was fun having
er kind of like a pet. But I don't think it's such a
good idea."

"Are you going to feed her again?" Robert asked
on the way home. "Can I bring stuff for her?"

"I'm coming back next weekend," Sandra
answered. "You can try to feed her then, if you
want."

Robert never got the chance. When he returned
with Sandra a week later, there were no pelicans at
the waterfall.

Chapter 21

The bus to Big River stopped at a gas station on the edge of town. Sandra jumped off the bottom step as her grandmother came out of the coffee shop.

"I'm back!" Sandra shouted.

Grandma Betty laughed. "Yes, finally. Your old friends have been asking about you. Let's get your stuff home, and then you can do some visiting. My car's around the side."

When they were driving, Sandra turned to her grandmother. "I like your hair," she said.

"Do you? I always like it short in the summer." Grandma Betty pulled at the dark brown strands. "Especially if I'm going camping."

"Camping?"

"Yes, I've been thinking that the two of us might go up to Kettle Lake for a couple of weeks. Do you remember Kettle Lake?"

sort of," Sandra answered. "I think I was there once with you and dad, when I was just little."

"That's right. We haven't been there for a few years."

"You used to live there, didn't you?"

"A long time ago. Before your dad was even born. I think you'll like it. It's a wonderful place in the summer."

"What's it like?"

"Well," Grandma Betty answered, "there's the lake, of course. And the forest all around. there are lots of places to visit and explore."

"Will it be just the two of us?"

"Yes. We'll have our own little cabin. And a boat and motor. Some fishing tackle."

"Sounds like fun!" Sandra said, "Do you think we'll see any wild animals?"

"Oh, probably. We used to see lots of game when we lived up there. That reminds me, Sandra. Whatever happened to that pelican of yours?"

"She's fine. She made it through the winter okay. When the rest of her flock came back in May, she joined them when they went up north. At least, I think she did. I never saw her by the waterfall any more. Hey, maybe I'll see her this summer!"

"Don't bet on it Sandra. I don't remember ever seeing pelicans on Kettle Lake."

When the time came to leave for Kettle Lake, Sandra helped her grandmother load their supplies into the back of a pickup truck. A friend of Grandma Betty's drove them on the four-hour trip north to Patuanak, a small settlement on the Churchill River.

Raising her voice over the sound of the motor Sandra asked, "What did you do when you lived at Kettle Lake, Grandma?"

Grandma Betty looked out the side window of the truck cab. "We were really young then, your grandpa and I. We wanted to live on our own, without any help from anyone. so we went to live in the bush. We built a little cabin, and just kind of lived off the land. We caught lots of fish. We trapped animals and sold the furs for a little income."

"Did you like it?"

"Oh, yes, I really liked living like that."

"How come you left?" Sandra asked.

Grandma Betty sighed. "We started having kids. It got to be too hard to raise children in the bush. So we moved down to Big River, which wasn't so bad. At that time, Big River was just a few houses, some stores, and the sawmill. That's where your grandpa worked, at the sawmill, just like your dad."

"You must miss Kettle Lake."

"I do. That's why I go back once in a while. To see the lake," Grandma Betty glanced at the man driving the truck, "and to visit with some of my friends, like Harvey here."

Harvey tugged at the peak of his red baseball cap. Written across the front of the cap were the words, Kettle Lake Lodge. As he drove, a faint smile curled the ends of his lips.

"I don't remember staying in a cabin when I was there with Dad," Sandra went on. "I thought we slept in a tent."

"We did," Grandma Betty answered. "Our old cabin fell down a long time ago. It's all rotted away, and trees have grown up where it used to be. But Harvey has a lodge on the lake. We're going to be

83

ing at one of his cabins this time."

At Patuanak, Harvey loaded their boxes and acks into a large freighter boat and passed each of them a bright orange life-jacket. The roar of the outboard motor kept anyone from talking for the two hours it took to get to his lodge. When they arrived, it was nearly dark. As two men unloaded the boat, Harvey led Sandra and Grandma Betty into the dining room for a late supper.

The next morning Sandra went down to the lake shore. A dock, its deck boards turned grey with age, moored a cluster of red and white boats. The wind rocked the boats against the dock and tossed Sandra's hair off her neck.

Sandra sat cross-legged at the end of the dock. Further down the shore, she could see someone hanging washing on a line, the sheets snapping in the breeze. Huge grey and white clouds raced across the sky. Out in the lake the water looked dark green.

Harvey had one of his workers load their supplies back into a boat. "I'll go up with you," he told Grandma Betty. "Eldon here will come up in another boat. When I see you're all fixed up, he and I will come back. and you'll be on your own!"

Along the shore of the lake, huge boulders lay scattered like broken sets of giant blocks. Steep cliffs covered in pale green lichens towered high as the tree tops. The light green leaves of poplar and birch trees stood out from the dark green needles of the pines.

"This is so pretty!" Sandra said, as the boat drifted onto a gravel shore near a small log cabin.

"That's why your grandpa and I stayed so long, Grandma Betty said.

"And why I never left," Harvey added. "I think you'll find everything you need here, Betty. You two go up and look around. Eldon and I'll unload your gear."

Half of the cabin was one open room. Near the centre stood a wood stove that could be used for cooking and heating. The wall that divided the cabin had two doors, each leading to a bedroom. One corner of the open room was a kitchen, with cupboards, a counter, and an icebox. Opening the cupboard doors, Sandra found the shelves well stocked with plates and pots and pans.

"Everything look all right?" Harvey asked, coming through the door.

"Couldn't be better," Grandma Betty said. "This is luxury we only dreamed about in the old days."

"Well, if you need anything, you know where the lodge is," he said. "We'll be getting back now. I'll drop by in a few days to see how you're doing."

Later, when she was helping her grandmother unpack, Sandra stopped to sniff the air. "What's that smoky smell?" she asked.

"I smelled that, too," Grandma Betty said. "It could be from a forest fire." She shook her head. "Don't worry, Sandra, it must be a long ways off or Harvey would have mentioned it."

Chapter 22

With each step, Sandra sank to her shins into a springy green carpet. Sometimes, at the bottom of a step, icy cold water flooded into her runners. Behind her, the carpet puffed back to fill in each footprint.

"What is this stuff?" Sandra asked, giggling.

"Sphagnum moss," Grandma Betty answered. "Isn't it something?" She stopped, bent down, and laced her fingers into the top of the carpet. "It's made up of million of these stringy little tubes that are all connected to each other."

Sandra patted the top of the moss. "If it wasn't so wet underneath, it would make a great bed. It's like a huge mattress."

"Right. It's like a sponge, too, when it's dry. Years ago, the Cree people around here used this for diapers."

Grandma Betty straightened up. "Let's head

toward that hill. It looks like there's a clearing on the other side." She held up a small hatchet she was carrying. "Do you want to use this now?"

"Sure," Sandra said. Taking the hatchet, she nicked some bark from a tree beside her. "How often do I do this?"

"Oh, every twenty-five steps or so. We don't want to get lost out here."

They climbed out of the mossy patch to the top of a steep ridge. Before them was a small lake, maybe three hundred metres across. A broad, flat, grey-speckled rock stretched from the top of the ridge to the water's edge. Across the lake, a family of ducks fed in some reeds.

"Perfect!" Grandma Betty sighed. She sat on the rock and untied the laces on her shoes. "Don't let me fall asleep," she murmured as she lay back against the sun-warmed rock. "We have to get back before too long. Harvey's dropping by for tea."

Harvey brought the news of the fire. "Have you been smelling that smoke?" he asked, as he came up the path to the cabin.

Grandma Betty nodded. "Yesterday it got pretty thick. Where's the fire?"

"Up by Cree Lake. It's a big one, and it's moving pretty fast. They're calling up extra crews, I guess." Harvey looked at Sandra. "That's quite a ways away. We're not in any danger here."

Grandma Betty folded her arms tightly across her chest. "I know what they say about these big fires keeping forests healthy in the long run. But I still don't like them."

"A forest fire is a terrible thing," Harvey agreed, sipping his tea. "When it's dry like it is up here this

mer, Sandra, the trees are just like torches
ady to be lit. All it takes to get things going is
maybe a flash of lightning or a cigarette that's not
put out.

"A spark might land on a bottom branch, and,"
Harvey snapped his fingers, "just like that a great
ball of flame rushes up the tree. At the top the fire-
ball explodes with a big whump! Sparks and smoke
blast off in all directions. And everywhere a spark
lands, another fire starts."

Sandra had heard stories like this before. She
wished he'd stop, but Harvey just took another sip
of tea and went right on. "Sometimes a fire might
get blocked by a small lake or some solid rock. But
even that doesn't stop it. These missiles get
launched from the treetops and before long sparks
drop down on the other side of whatever's blocking
the fire, and new fires start. That's what a forest
fire is – lots of fires and plenty of thick, hot smoke."

Sandra was nibbling at the edges of a cookie.
"Can the animals get away?" she asked.

"Some of them do," Harvey answered. "A lot of
them are killed, of course. They get trapped by the
flames or they're choked by that awful smoke."

Frowning, Sandra asked, "What about birds, like
ducks and loons, that live on a lake? What would
they do?

"I expect most birds would fly off somewhere,
away from the smoke," Harvey said. "Some might
not be able to make it. And I suppose birds that
were raising babies might have to leave their little
ones behind."

"That would be terrible," Sandra said.

"Actually," Harvey said, with a happier note in
his voice, "that's what I really came to tell you

about. There are some new birds on our lake. Pelicans. I figure they must have been driven here by the fire."

Chapter 23

After finishing her breakfast chores the next morning, Sandra went down to the lake. The boat had been pulled bow-first onto the beach. Sandra climbed in. Sitting on the middle seat and staring across the lake, she didn't hear her grandmother come down the path.

"So?" Grandma Betty asked, leaning against the boat. "You're kind of quiet."

"I'm thinking about those pelicans Harvey told us about," Sandra answered.

"I thought you might be," Grandma Betty said. "Think we should go check them out?"

"Yes!"

"We could. Not because I think your pelican is one of them, mind you. But it's probably time we took a trip around the lake anyway. Let's put together a little lunch. We can look for a spot for a picnic."

Sandra jumped out of the boat as her grandmother turned back to the cabin. "Harvey says there's an eagle's nest down at the end of the lake now," Grandma Betty said. "That would be worth a trip by itself."

A short time later, they pulled on their life-jackets and loaded a pack into the boat. After pushing away from the shore, Sandra pulled her dripping feet over the bow.

Grandma Betty grasped the cord to start the outboard motor. A sharp pull brought the motor to life. She slipped it into gear, turned around to face the front, and twisted the handle. The bow lifted out of the water as the speed and noise of the motor increased.

It didn't take long to find the pelicans. Their tall white bodies could be seen clearly from far down the lake. While their boat was still a long way off, Grandma Betty shut off the motor and they paddled close to the flock. The pelicans were floating a few metres out from the rocky shoreline.

After counting the birds, Sandra said quietly, "You're right, Grandma. This isn't Pelly's flock. It isn't big enough. Can I try to feed them, anyway?"

"Might as well," Grandma Betty said. "Hold on." She let the boat drift to shore around a corner from the flock. Sandra jumped over the side and pulled the boat onto a little beach. When she glanced back, Grandma Betty waved her away.

From rock to rock, Sandra slowly picked her way along the shoreline toward the pelicans. As she got closer, Sandra saw that one of the birds swam apart from the rest of the flock. When she was about twenty metres from the birds, she crouched down and called softly, "Hi pelicans! I have some od for you."

Startled, the pelicans beat their winds and skimmed further out into the lake. The lone bird flapped its wings, but didn't fly away.

"Pelly, is that you?" Sandra asked.

Tucking its bill against its neck, the pelican stared at Sandra.

"It is you, isn't it?" Sandra stood slowly. "Watch this, Pelly." Balancing on a flat rock, Sandra stretched her arms wide.

The pelican continued to stare for a moment. Then she arched her wings out to their full length.

"Wow!" Sandra whispered. "I can't believe this. My grandma and I are staying at a cabin just down the lake. and now you've come for a visit."

From her jacket pocket, Sandra pulled bits of bread for the pelican. When she had picked up all the bread, Pelly paddled slowly along the shore.

Sandra followed.

"Is this really all that's left of your flock? Is it because you got caught in the fire?" Sandra asked. "You guys look pretty droopy. Maybe I should bring you more stuff. I'll get Grandma to come back tomorrow."

As Pelly arched her wings, Sandra stopped and again spread her arms wide. "See you," she said. The pelican swam out to her flock.

Chapter 24

And then I never saw her again," Sandra explained to her father. She was back in Saskatoon, waiting for school to start. "The next day," she went on, "there was a big storm. It rained really hard, and there were whitecaps on the lake. It was two days before we could get in the boat and go look for the pelicans. By then they were gone."

"That's too bad," Wesley said, "especially if you think your pelican was in that flock."

"It was Pelly, I know it was," Sandra said.

"Did you look anywhere else?" Wesley pulled on his moustache. "Maybe the pelicans just went somewhere else on the lake."

"We went all around the lake. We even stopped at Harvey's lodge to see if they'd seen the pelicans again, but no-one had."

"So, now you'll have to wait to see them at the

waterfall again."

Sandra smiled. "This is when I saw Pelly last year. Boy! that seems like a long time ago. Now when she comes it'll be just like seeing an old friend."

"Right," Wesley said. "Say, speaking of old friends, have you seen Jason and Robert yet?"

"Yes. I gave each of them one of the eagle feathers I found at the lake."

"Did they like them?"

"They were really impressed. Jason said he'd keep his wherever they went. That's when I found out – they're moving."

"Really?"

"Their mom's got a job in Yorkton," Sandra said. "Jason says he doesn't mind moving. They've lived there before, 1 guess. This time they're going to have a house of their own."

"They'll like that all right. When are they moving?"

"At the end of September," Sandra said. "I wish they didn't have to go so soon."

The first weeks of school passed quickly. On the day that Jason and Robert were going to move, the boys piled boxes and furniture on the small lawn in front of the apartment building. Sandra came outside to find Robert sitting on a kitchen chair. In his hand he was holding a large sheet of white paper, rolled tightly.

"We can't find him anywhere," Robert said in a worried voice. "I've been all down the street and the back alleys. I checked all his favourite places."

"Maybe he doesn't want to move," Sandra said.

"Well, if he doesn't show up right away," Jason

said, stacking a suitcase on top of a chair, "Mom says we have to leave without him. Will you watch out for him, Sandra? He's just a stupid stray cat, but I don't want him starving to death."

"Sure, I'll watch for him," Sandra said. "Anyway, he's not stupid, he's a nice cat."

"Aw, he's okay," Jason said. "Not like that pelican, though. That was something. Did it ever come back?"

Sandra frowned. "No, not yet. But she'll be here any day. I guess I'll be waiting around for two pets now!"

"Well," Jason said, "I know which one I'd rather take with me."

Looking down at the ground, Robert swung his heel against a chair leg, kicking it again and again.

"It's all right, Robert," Sandra said. "No Pets will be okay. He's just the kind of cat that likes to be by himself sometimes. If he shows up after you're gone, I'll find him a good home. So, what's that in your hand?"

Robert looked at the roll of white paper as if it had just been handed to him. "I forgot. This is for you. But you can't open it until we're gone."

Chapter 25

Sandra was alone on the riverbank until a man wearing a green toque walked up beside her.

"They're usually here by now, aren't they?" the man asked.

Too surprised to speak, Sandra looked up at her visitor.

"Hi, Sandra," he went on. "Remember me?"

"Of course. You're Ernie, from the fish store. What are you doing here?"

"Oh, I was just sort of passing by, and I saw you sitting here. May I join you?"

"Sure."

As Ernie sat down, he lay a plastic bag on the ground beside him. Pulling his arms around his knees, he nudged up his glasses with his shoulder. "I meant the pelicans. They usually come in September and stay for a while, don't they?"

"I think so."

"Say, whatever happened to that pelican friend of yours?" Ernie asked. "Did it stay here all summer?"

"She went up north, with her flock."

Raising his eyebrows, Ernie asked, "Now, how do you know that?"

"I saw her this summer," Sandra said.

"No! Where did you see her?" Sounding like he didn't believe Sandra, he asked, "How could you tell it was the same one?"

"I was at Kettle lake with my grandma. Pelly came there once with her flock. There weren't as many as there were down here. They were chased to Kettle Lake by the forest fires."

Sandra paused. She poked a hole in the ground with a small twig. "I know it was her, because we have a special signal. She waves to me, and I wave back."

Ernie looked over at Sandra. "Is that right? You really did get to know that pelican, didn't you?" He rubbed his chin. "It must have been pretty rough up north with all the fires. Did the pelicans stay on that lake then?"

"No, they left right away," Sandra answered. "There was a storm, and when it was over they'd all gone. I don't know where they went. Now I wish she'd stayed here all summer. At least then I'd know she was okay."

"I know what you mean," Ernie said. "But I'm sure you did the right thing by not trying to keep the pelican where it didn't want to be."

Sandra was quiet. There was a strong smell of fish in the air. Maybe, she thought, Ernie always smelled like the fish store.

Turning to Sandra, Ernie asked in a serious voice, "Did you see any turtles where you were this summer?"

Seeing Sandra shake her head, Ernie went on. "Maybe you were too far north. You can sometimes see them around here, though. You might find one sunning on a log or a stone. Sometimes they get this big." He held up his hands to show something about the size of a large dinner plate. "Or bigger. Greeny-brown on the top, but beautiful designs of red and black and yellow and brown on the bottom.

"When I was a kid, I caught a turtle once," he continued. "I had it kind of cornered on the river-bank. I figured if I flipped it over it couldn't get away."

Sandra watched Ernie closely. He tugged at his toque. "Well, I got it flipped over with a stick. Right away it pulled in its head and feet, so there was just the shell. And then I saw all these wild colours on its underside. Just like you'd taken a brush and painted them on. I put my finger on its belly and started tracing the lines.

"I must have tickled it or something, because all of a sudden this little head comes shooting out of the shell. Then these big pinchers open up and it takes a chomp on my finger.

"I jerked my hand back really quick. You can guess what happened, eh? This," he said, and waved his hand with the one cut-off finger.

Sandra giggled. She knew now it was another one of Ernie's stories.

"Hey," Ernie acted shocked, "it's not funny. It really hurt!"

"I'm sure," Sandra laughed. "How many stories do you have about that short finger, anyway?"

"Oh, about one a day," Ernie said and grinned. He stood up and brushed the back of his pants. "Anyway, I'd better get going."

"Me, too," Sandra said, standing. "I have to get home." She looked at the bag in Ernie's hand. The bottom was stretched out, as if whatever was inside was heavy. It reminded Sandra of the bags she used to carry to Pelly.

"You know," Ernie said, swinging the bag behind his back, "I'm going to keep coming to watch for those pelicans. Maybe I'll see you down here again."

"That'd be nice" Sandra smiled. "Except I can't come as much as I did last year."

"No? How come?"

Sandra shrugged. "None of my friends are really that interested. And they get mad if I come here and wait for Pelly instead of playing with them."

"That's too bad," Ernie said. "but it won't be long before the pelicans are here, and you can visit with your special one. And then they'll all fly off south, and you'll have time for your friends. Right?" He paused, "Or do you think your pelican will stay here all winter again?"

"I don't know," Sandra answered. "But I know what I wish she'd do."

"We'll find out pretty soon," Ernie said. "So long, Sandra."

"See you."

Ernie turned to walk down a path. With him went the smell of fish.

Chapter 26

Two and three at a time, the pelicans glided down to the waterfall. Just above the water, each bird stuck out its legs, held back its wings, and skied across the top of the waves. Pulling in its wings, each pelican settled into the river.

As if following orders, the birds quickly formed groups to fish together below the falls.

Two boys watched the pelicans from a path near the weir. Each stood with one foot on the ground and the other hooked over the bar of his bicycle. As they spoke, the wind seemed to pull thin streams of white breath from their mouths.

"This time we get one, right?" one boy said.

"Yeah," the redhead answered, "we will. My uncle's got a pellet gun I can use. I can get it whenever I want."

"How far does it shoot?"

"Halfway across the river. One of them just has

to come close to shore and I'll bag it, easy."

"Hey, my dad's got some new duck waders," the first boy said. "I bet I can use them. We won't even have to get wet."

"Okay, but we've got to move it." the redhead said, sliding onto the seat of his bike. "These birds aren't going to stick around very long."

Riding along beside the redhead, the other boy laughed. "This'll be a cinch! I already know what I'm going to buy with that twenty-five bucks."

From her apartment window a few blocks away, Sandra could see the sky above the river. Discouraged by weeks of waiting, she dropped, knees first, onto the couch. Except for some fast-moving grey clouds, the sky was empty.

Beside the window a picture of a pelican was taped to the wall. It was Robert's present. He had printed "Pelly" at the bottom. As she glanced at the picture, Sandra remembered how the boys had envied her friendship with the pelican.

A movement in the backyard tree caught her attention. It was No Pets. The big yellow cat was staring at her while slowly swinging his tail beneath a branch.

"You're back!" Sandra laughed. In a few moments she was in the yard waving at No Pets.

"Where've you been?" she called. "I thought you were long gone, you silly cat."

Stepping over a pile of leaves, Sandra walked closer to the tree. No Pets slunk along the branch toward her.

"Are you looking for a new home? Maybe you can stay with us, if you behave yourself. Come on down!" Sandra rubbed her arms. And hurry up.

It's freezing out here!"

A gust of wind swirled through the yard, blowing Sandra's hair across her face. Behind her, leaves danced around the pile, then lay down. Raising his hind legs slightly, No Pets tensed to jump.

"Not like that!" Sandra cried.

No Pets sprang, sailing over Sandra's head. Leaves scattered from the pile as he landed, legs out, with a soft thud. Sandra picked up the limp cat and hung him over her shoulder. Gently stroking his back, she walked into the building.

By the time Sandra reached her apartment, No Pets was purring. She laid him on the couch. As she straightened up, Sandra saw through the window two white birds soaring in wide circles.

"The pelicans!" she exclaimed. "I've got to go, No Pets. I'll talk to my dad about you when he comes home. You wait here." She grabbed her jacket from a hook and ran from the apartment.

A few minutes later Sandra slipped, out of breath, down the riverbank. The flock of pelicans was lifting off the water. She watched the birds make a large arc. They started to the north along the river. Then they turned west, and finally, as the birds flew over the river again, they headed off to the south. Each pelican in the line flapped its wings in time with the leader, then glided on the air currents. Sandra could count only twenty birds.

Is that all there are? she wondered. Sandra quickly searched the river below the falls. There were no more pelicans.

The flock was right over Sandra. Throwing back her head, she tried to find one pelican that might be Pelly.

I can't tell, she thought, as tears welled up in

her eyes. They all look the same.

The birds seemed to grow smaller as they flew higher and higher. Sandra sighed deeply. I should have come down sooner, she told herself. Now I've missed her.

When the flock reached the far shore of the river, a single pelican veered off toward the railway bridge. the bird glided down to a man that Sandra hadn't noticed standing on the walkway.

Just above the man, the bird pushed its wings backwards. It seemed to almost stop in mid-air. The man shifted a white plastic bag from his right hand to his left and waved it at the pelican.

Beating its wings again, the pelican turned and dived down to Sandra. The bird splashed softly into the water.

Sandra crouched in the mud. Hugging her arms around her knees, she spoke in quick bursts. "I thought I'd missed you, Pelly! I felt terrible! Thanks for coming to say goodbye. But you'd better get going. I don't want you to be left behind again!"

With her bill pressed against her neck, Pelly stared at the girl.

Frowning, Sandra said, "you're not going to stay again, are you?"

Pelly remained still in the water. Her feet paddled steadily to keep her near Sandra.

"Pelly, you have to go! You –" Sandra laughed. "I know what you're doing, you old mooch, you're waiting for some food!"

Sandra slipped her hand into her jacket pocket and tossed some bread crumbs to the pelican. Swimming closer to shore, Pelly picked the crumbs from the water. Then she beat her wings once.

"You ready to go now?" Sandra asked. "Good!

You'd better hurry!"

Spreading her arms wide, Sandra went up on tiptoe. Pelly arched her wings and pulled herself partly out of the water.

"I'll be thinking of you all winter," Sandra said. "And I'll be right here waiting for you when you come back!"

The pelican turned, and with a few quick wing strokes, rose high above the river. She kept beating her wings, with a few rests, until she had reached the flock and taken her place in the line.

"So long, Pelly," Sandra said. Then she turned and waved to the lone figure on the bridge.

Ernie smiled, and waved back.

About the author, Dave Glaze

Dave Glaze has spent fifteen years as a teacher, teacher-librarian, and educational consultant. He has also worked as a writer/editor for a number of organizations, including the Saskatchewan Environmental Society. He lives in Saskatoon, Saskatchewan with his wife and two daughters.

About the illustrator, Bill Johnson

Bill Johnson is a former librarian who currently designs and illustrates books. He has lived in almost every province in Canada, and now resides in Nelson, British Columbia.